The Imaginary Day

By May Lee-Yang

Illustrations by Anne Sawyer-Aitch

About the Reading Together Project:

The Reading Together Project seeks to address the lack of children's books that speak to the experience of being an Asian Pacific Islander (API) child or youth in the United States. The project supports the development of English literacy skills while recognizing cultural heritage, and creating opportunities for children and families to learn about API cultural heritage together.

Book design: Kim Jackson, Dalros Design
Copy editor: Sally Heuer
Proof editor: Eden Bart
Printed by: Grace Wong with Team One Printing

ISBN: 978-0-9884539-1-3

10 9 8 7 6 5 4 3 2 1
First Edition

Contents

[Dedication]

For my nephews Soriyu and Shawn, who inspired this book;
Payton and Noah, who will eventually get their own books;
and the many other nieces and nephews who have blessed my life

[Acknowledgments]

This project would not have been possible without the support of many wonderful people. Thank you to my husband, Peter, who helped with late-night brainstorming and reminders to keep the story fun; illustrator Anne Sawyer-Aitch for bringing this world into life; Sally Heuer for insightful editing; Ilean Her for spearheading this project; and Kham Vang, Junauda Petrus, Casey DeMarais, and the rest of the Minnesota Humanities Center staff for all of their administrative support. Thank you for giving my imagination an opportunity to connect my past with my present.

[CHAPTER 1]

The First Day
of Summer Vacation

The first day of summer vacation started out lame.

The trouble began at breakfast when no one wanted to eat anything that Mom cooked.

"I want pancakes," said Payton. She was three years old, the only girl in the family, and, therefore, the princess.

"We don't have any pancakes," said Mom.

On the kitchen table, she set a big bowl of steaming jasmine rice next to baked chicken wings, stir-fried vegetables, and a small bowl of chili pepper sauce. Mostly, the chili pepper sauce was for Mom. She and other adults liked to use it for dipping, but the kids knew she often kept it around to threaten them.

"If you say bad words, you're eating the pepper," she always said. Or, "If you fight with your siblings, you're eating the pepper."

"If Payton gets pancakes, I want to eat my favorite food in the entire world," said Noah. "I want to eat noodles with no broth, no spoon, no water. I only want a fork and a glass of milk."

Noah had just turned five years old and graduated from preschool, so he thought he was a big boy now. He was also a ninja-in-training and believed in making sure everyone was equal. That meant if Payton got special food, so should he.

"Can I get Hmong sausages then?" asked Tou Bee. He was eight years old and went to a special Hmong charter school where they ate sticky rice and Hmong sausages for breakfast all the time.

"There will be no pancakes, no noodles, and no Hmong sausages for breakfast," said Mom. "Back in the day, when I was your age—"

And before she could continue, everyone groaned. Mom was always talking about "back in the day."

"Back in the day," Mom continued, "I ate whatever Grandma and Grandpa made. I didn't complain. Back then, if you didn't eat, you starved."

"But, Mom, I'm a princess," Payton reminded her, and Mom groaned.

"No pancakes. No noodles. No sausages. And, by the way, where is Tou Cher?"

Tou Cher was Tou Bee's twin, though the two of them didn't look identical. They were fraternal twins. That was why Tou Bee had a big head with small ears, and Tou Cher had a small head with big ears. They evened each other out.

"He's still sleeping," said Tou Bee. He always answered for Tou Cher when his brother was not there.

"Go wake him up to eat," said Mom. Then she eyed the small bowl of chili pepper sauce. Today it looked like someone might be eating pepper after all.

• • •

[CHAPTER 2]

The Problem

[★]

After breakfast, Mom said, "I'm going to do the dishes, and then we'll all spend some quality time together."

Mom was a high school teacher, so she was always busy during the school year. But that also meant she had summers free to hang out with her kids.

Everyone filed into the living room, and right away Tou Bee and Tou Cher turned on the TV and started playing *The Awesome Adventures of Avery the Elf King* on the Wii. They had been playing the game every day after school for two weeks now, and they were getting close to the end, where Avery had to battle a gigantic dragon.

Payton turned on her iPod and put on her glass princess shoes, which were really just plastic. Then she started dancing. Against the hardwood floors, her shoes made a loud click-clacking noise.

Noah went straight to the computer.

"You guys, how do you get video games on the computer?" he asked. Even though he was a big boy now and knew his ABC's, he couldn't spell things like "Dragon Ball Z" or "Nickelodeon" on the computer. So he always had to ask someone to help him spell.

But everyone was too busy to pay attention to him.

When Mom entered the living room, she stopped in her tracks. Payton was click-clacking around the living room, knocking down framed pictures, vases, and anything in her path; Tou Bee and Tou Cher had their eyes glued to the TV, their hands gripping the video game controllers; and Noah's loud voice kept saying, "How do you get video games on the computer? How do you get video games on the computer? How do you get video games on the computer?"

It was as loud as the Hmong New Year!

"Everyone, quiet down," said Mom.

But no one heard her.

"Payton, stop dancing. Tou Bee and Tou Cher, lower the volume on the TV. Noah, I will get to you in a moment."

And still no one heard her.

Then Mom yelled, "ENOUGH!" and *that* got everyone's attention because Mom didn't yell…Well, not very much anyway. She was the nice teacher at her school. She even had a card from her students that said so. But right now Mom's face was red, her mouth made a thin line, and her eyes squinted. She was mad.

"I have an idea," Mom said with a sudden smile that made everyone scared. "I have decided that for this entire day, you will all say good-bye to technology."

No one said anything at first. Then Noah asked, "What's technology?"

"It's your iPod, video games, and computer."

At that, everyone yelled, "No! What are we supposed to do for the rest of the day? Summer vacation is gonna be so boring. Can't we just eat some pepper?"

"Back in the day," said Mom, and she held up her hand before anyone could groan, "we didn't have any of these things, but we had fun anyway."

"What did you do?" asked Tou Bee.

"Well, we played cops and robbers with the neighbor kids."

Tou Bee scrunched his face. He didn't like being active.

"We played Hmong games like stick and ball."

That sounds kind of boring, thought Payton.

"We hunted for crayfish at creeks and ponds."

Lame, thought Tou Cher with a shrug.

"One time, I brought home a cat and tried to raise it without telling my parents."

"Ooh, that sounds like fun!" said Noah.

"But *don't* do that," said Mom. "Back in the day, we didn't have all the things you have now, but we had something better than a TV or iPod or computer."

All the kids leaned in, waiting to hear what this wondrous, magical thing was.

"We had an imagination," said Mom.

An imagination? thought all the kids. *What was fun about an imagination?*

• • •

[CHAPTER 3]

The Quest

[★]

Playing with your imagination isn't very fun, thought Tou Cher. Mom was teaching them how to play stick and ball on the living room floor. She got ten pencils and one lime because she couldn't find a ball.

"First, you throw the ball in the air," she began.

"You mean the lime," said Noah, because he always liked things to be correct.

"Yes," said Mom. "First you throw the lime in the air, then you grab a pencil before the lime can fall to the ground."

"Well, what do you do with the lime?" asked Payton.

"You grab it after you get the pencil," said Tou Bee. He had played this game many times at Hmong school. If Tou Cher hadn't gotten so many time-outs in class, he would have known this game too.

"Then what happens after that?" asked Payton.

"You repeat it until all the pencils are picked up," said Mom.

"Lame."

Tou Cher said those words under his breath, but Mom heard them anyway. Her ears were as sharp as a dragon's even though he wasn't sure if dragons actually had ears, and anyway, she was a teacher. She was used to hearing children mutter under their breaths.

"That wasn't a very nice thing to say," said Mom, and for a moment, Tou Cher thought he saw sparks of fire in her brown eyes. He shook it off, thinking maybe it was just his imagination.

"I'm bored," he said.

"You're always bored," said Mom.

It was true. That was why he always talked in class. Or told jokes. Or did stuff he wasn't supposed to do.

"Can't we just play *The Awesome Adventures of Avery the Elf King*? We're almost at the end of the game."

"What's so great about *The Awesome Adventures of Avery*?" asked Mom.

"The hero, Avery, is just a regular boy," began Tou Cher.

"But then he learns he's king of the elves," said Tou Bee.

"You get to battle ogres," said Tou Cher.

"But it's also very educational," added Tou Bee. "You have to solve puzzles."

Mom pasted on one of her fake smiles, the one she wore when she thought something wasn't that funny but you had to pretend to like it was anyway so you didn't hurt the feelings of other people.

"No more video games today. Why don't you boys go play in the backyard?" said Mom. "It's summer. You can be active. Wouldn't that be fun?"

"Okay," said Tou Bee, because he always liked to make sure Mom was happy. Tou Cher looked at the Wii one more time, but the actual video game disc was gone. In fact, all their video games were gone. Mom hid them right before teaching the lame stick-and-ball game.

"If you don't want to go outside, I could teach you some more games from back in the day," said Mom with a smile.

That did it. Tou Cher slumped his shoulders and shuffled to the backyard. This was going to be the most boring summer ever. The only good thing was that Mom kept the little kids in the house with her.

In the backyard, Tou Bee asked, "You wanna throw a football around?" If Tou Bee had to be active, he threw balls, because this meant you only had to stand in one spot.

Tou Cher shrugged. He liked shrugging. It was a cool way to say, "sure." But if you didn't want to do something, shrugging could also mean, "not really."

Throwing the football around was only fun for five minutes. Then he got bored again.

"You wanna play catch?" asked Tou Bee, holding up a baseball.

Tou Cher shrugged again, and they played catch. But

before five minutes was up, they lost the ball. Tou Cher had thrown it over the fence. Oh, it wasn't an accident. He was trying to see how far and how high the ball could go.

It went pretty far, he thought. "I'm gonna go get the ball," he said. He started walking toward the gate that opened into the back alley of their house when Tou Bee stopped him.

"Remember when Mom said we couldn't go back there without her? I'll just go get Mom."

"Don't bother her," said Tou Cher. "I'll go get it."

Actually, he liked to bother Mom sometimes. When he was bored and stuck in the house, he liked to break stuff, or poke Noah, or hide Payton's toys just to see what Mom would say. Right now, though, he wanted to get out of the yard. Being active wasn't that fun when you only had one person to play with and the sun was baking you like a chicken. And Tou Cher was no chicken.

"I don't think you should open the gate," said Tou Bee.

"Why are you always so scared of getting in trouble?"

asked Tou Cher. "You're the good twin. Everyone knows that."

"And why do you always have to do bad things?" asked Tou Bee.

"I don't do bad things," said Tou Cher. "I'm just... curious."

And with that, he opened the gate anyway and found...

Nothing.

Just the ball sitting on the grass. Tou Cher poked his head into the alley. He looked right and left. He expected to see a black cat at the very least, but there was nothing.

"That does it," he said to Tou Bee. "We're going to look for our video games."

"But Mom said—"

"I don't think she's Mom anymore, Tou Bee. When she was talking to me earlier, she had these weird eyes."

"What weird eyes?"

"I saw flames."

"*Flames*?" Tou Bee didn't look like he believed his brother.

But Tou Cher's imagination was already working. "Mom *is* so nice," he said.

"Yes, she *is* very nice," agreed Tou Bee. "She even got an award from her school for being the nicest teacher."

"And she would never do something mean like take away our video games."

"You might be right," said Tou Bee, considering this.

"So, let's go look for our games."

"But we don't know where she hid them."

"We can do this," said Tou Cher. "We're good at solving mysteries. Like Avery the elf king."

"Yes, we could be like Avery."

And just like that, Tou Cher knew he had changed Tou Bee's mind.

• • •

[CHAPTER 4]

The Stash

[★]

Everyone knows that before you start an adventure, you have to get supplies. In *The Awesome Adventures of Avery the Elf King*, Avery always went to different villages to get food, weapons, and maps.

Tou Bee and Tou Cher went to the kitchen.

First, they made sure no one was around. Then they opened the fridge.

"What do you think we'll need on our adventure?" asked Tou Bee.

"Everything," said Tou Cher. He opened some drawers and used them as stairs to get onto the kitchen counter.

Tou Bee opened his backpack and threw in juice boxes and apples. He saw some leftover chicken wings and dumped them into his backpack as well.

From behind him, Tou Cher screamed, "Oh yeah!"

"What is it?" asked Tou Bee.

Tou Cher pointed to the cabinet in the highest corner of the kitchen. "The secret stash," he said in awe.

Tou Bee's eyes were ready to bug out. He saw bags of potato chips, jars of candy, and containers of cookies. The only thing missing for Tou Bee was Hmong sausages.

"Come on. Help me get some," said Tou Cher.

Tou Bee dragged a chair to the kitchen counter—it was much safer than climbing on the drawers. Then he lifted himself onto the chair and jumped onto the countertop. He unzipped his backpack, but instead of throwing in more supplies, he opened a bag of potato chips and started munching on them. Tou Cher joined him. Because the potato chips were salty, the boys needed something to drink, so they opened the juice boxes.

"The cookies, we gotta eat the cookies too," said Tou Bee in between sips. The two of them munched down two cookies each before remembering to throw a few in their backpacks.

"What are you two doing?" asked a shocked voice.

They had been so busy eating they didn't even realize someone had entered the kitchen. Both boys turned toward the voice. Standing in the doorway was a dangerous-looking ninja. His whole face was covered, except for his eyes.

"We're going on an adventure," said Tou Bee.

"To eat everything in the kitchen?" asked the ninja.

When Tou Bee looked around, he saw crumbs, empty boxes, and candy wrappers everywhere. All the drawers and cabinet doors were open as well.

"You're not supposed to be eating anything until lunch," said the ninja, and with that, he disappeared out the door and up the stairs.

"He's gonna tattle on us," said Tou Cher. "Why can't he act more like a kid?"

But they knew it was because Noah liked rules, and the rules said, "No snacks until lunch."

"If he tattles on us, then Mom–or that thing that's pretending to be her–will come get us," said Tou Bee.

Upstairs, there were pitter-patter sounds across the floorboards. *The ninja!* The twins gave each other one quick look before they scrambled onto the ground.

"The evil Mom will be here soon," said Tou Cher.

"Where can we hide?"

Frantically, they looked around before spying a doorway. Without saying anything, they both ran toward the door.

"Wait! We need to make sure we have everything," said Tou Bee. "Do we have rope?"

"I found some yarn," said Tou Cher.

"That'll work. What about water? We may be gone for a very long time, and we'll need water."

"We still have juice boxes."

"Food?"

"Duh. What do you think we've been stuffing into our

backpacks this whole time?"

"What about—"

And before Tou Bee could finish his sentence, a loud *thud-thud-thud* sounded above them. The ninja had tattled on them.

"Time to go," said Tou Cher, and both of them dashed through the doorway.

• • •

[CHAPTER 5]

The Dungeon

[★]

As soon as the twins went through the doorway, darkness swallowed them.

"You led us into the dungeon!" cried Tou Bee.

Still, there was no turning back. The evil Mom was coming after them.

"So what?" said Tou Cher. "In *The Awesome Adventures of Avery the Elf King*, there's always stuff hidden in the dungeon."

Even Tou Bee had to agree with that. Still, he didn't want to lead the way into the darkness, even if he was older than Tou Cher by two minutes.

"I wish we had a flashlight," said Tou Bee.

"I have something even better," said Tou Cher, sifting through his backpack. "I have a torch."

Suddenly, a wonderful light glowed around Tou Cher's hands.

"That's a flashlight," said Tou Bee.

"I said it's a torch, so it's a torch," argued Tou Cher.

Tou Bee wanted to correct him, to point out that torches usually had fire burning at their end, but behind him the thud-thud-thud sound was much closer.

"Hurry, let's go hide," he whispered to Tou Cher. He didn't want to talk too loudly in case the ninja or Evil Mom was on the other side of the doorway.

Together, the twins took one step at a time. It wouldn't have been very smart to run headlong into the unknown. Finally, they walked off the last set of steps.

Tou Cher shined his torch all around to see what the room looked like. The ceilings were high. The floors were flat. As far as he could tell, there were no rats scurrying around.

Both Tou Cher and Tou Bee knew that dungeons were dark. But they never would have figured that a dungeon would be so well organized and clean. They were pretty sure that if it weren't so dark, they would see there were no cobwebs.

"The evil Mom probably scared away all the spiders," said Tou Cher.

The dungeon contained rows and rows of boxes lined up. All the boxes were labeled with things like "Halloween," "Christmas," and "old clothes."

"Where would she hide our games?" Tou Cher wondered out loud.

The boys decided to search the box marked "fun stuff" first. But when they opened the box, all they saw were stickers and tiny bottles of bubbles.

"Lame," said Tou Cher.

"The bubbles might come in handy," said Tou Bee, and he threw two bubble bottles in his backpack.

Next, they searched a box that said "toys." If their video games were hidden anywhere, surely they'd be among the toys. Tou Bee held up the torch while Tou

Cher opened the box.

As soon as he opened the flaps of the box, Tou Cher sighed again. "Lame."

Even Tou Bee had to admit that these toys were only good for babies. They found rattles, teddy bears, and blocks with letters of the alphabet.

"In *The Awesome Adventures of Avery the Elf King*, the bad guys are always tricky," said Tou Bee. "Maybe Mom—"

"You mean Evil Mom," said Tou Cher.

"Yes, Evil Mom. Maybe Evil Mom is sneaky. Maybe we should look somewhere we *wouldn't* expect video games to be."

Tou Cher's eyes widened with understanding.

"Man, we are smart," he said. "Who said video games don't teach you anything?"

He grabbed his flashlight—no, his torch—from Tou Bee and shined it around to better see the other labels on the boxes. Finally, against the back wall, on one of the highest shelves, he spotted what he was looking for. He was willing to bet their video games were hidden in the box marked "boring stuff."

The only problem was that the shelf was very high and he could only think of one way to get up there.

"Tou Bee, I need to climb on you," said Tou Cher.

"Why can't *I* climb on *you*?" asked Tou Bee.

"Because I'm smaller than you."

"No, you're not. Only my head is bigger than yours. And your ears are bigger than mine. We even each other out, remember?"

This was true. Everyone told them so. Still, Tou Cher wanted to be the one to get to the box. He secretly wanted to be the hero, the one who saved the day.

He was stuck, not sure what to say to Tou Bee, when an idea came to him.

"I get to climb on you because I'm younger than you.

By two minutes."

Tou Bee groaned because he knew it was true.

"Fine, fine, fine," said Tou Bee, getting on his hands and knees. He felt like a table. Or a dog. Or an older brother who always had to do things for his younger brother.

Tou Cher placed the torch next to his brother, then he climbed onto Tou Bee.

Tou Bee felt his brother's tennis shoes sink into his back. He waited for something to happen. And he waited.

"What are you doing up there?" he finally asked.

"The box is still too high," said Tou Cher.

When Tou Bee craned his neck to look up, he saw that Tou Cher only reached the second shelf, and the "boring stuff" box was on the third shelf.

"Then get off me!" said Tou Bee.

"Fine, fine, fine."

When Tou Cher finally got off Tou Bee, the two of them stared at the box and wondered how they might get up there. They walked back and forth, shining the torch all around the cavernous room and staring at all the boxes.

"What would Avery do?" wondered Tou Cher, thinking out loud.

In the game, this was usually the part where the two brothers were stuck for a while. They would enter a room where there were no doors to anywhere, but they knew *something* was supposed to happen.

"There's usually a puzzle to solve," said Tou Bee.

"But all we have in here are boxes," said Tou Cher.

"Boxes which could be..."

"Blocks!" both of them yelled before they remembered they needed to be quiet.

They looked at the rows and rows of boxes. If they pulled them out, they could build a staircase toward the "boring stuff" box.

Very quickly, they pulled two boxes off the shelves and onto the ground, making the first set of stairs. Tou Cher climbed on these. On the second shelf, Tou Cher pulled out another box, which immediately stacked onto the first boxes. This made the second set of stairs. He climbed higher.

This high up, he could actually reach the box of "boring stuff" if he stood on his toes.

"Get ready, Tou Bee. I'm gonna bring down the box."

Tou Cher got on his tippy-toes and tested the box. It felt a little heavy, but not that heavy. He was sure he could carry it on his own without any help from his brother.

He slid the box over the edge of the shelf. That was when the box fell and a flurry of paper flew all around them like leaves falling off a tree.

Tou Cher himself was about to fall from his perch

when he felt Tou Bee's hands steady him. It was good to know his brother was always there to catch him before he could fall.

The two boys scooted down their pretend steps and looked all around for a thin plastic box or a disc, anything that looked like a video game.

"It's nothing but paper," said Tou Bee.

"It really was a box of boring stuff," said Tou Cher.

But the twins didn't have very long to mope, because right then and there the dungeon door opened, a beam of orange light shone through the doorway, and Evil Mom's voice boomed, "WHO'S DOWN THERE DISTURBING MY DUNGEON?"

Though he knew it was a bad idea, Tou Cher scooted himself one shelf over to get a better view of Evil Mom. That was the problem with curiosity. You saw stuff you didn't want to see. What he saw was no longer Mom. At the top of the staircase, he saw the outline of a creature with wild hair and claws for hands.

"She's turning into a dragon," whispered Tou Bee next to him. Tou Bee must have gotten enough courage to be curious too.

"What should we do?" asked Tou Bee.

"Get out of here!" answered Tou Cher. He couldn't stop himself from saying, "Duh."

But the only way out was through the dungeon door where Evil Mom still stood. Then more light flooded the dungeon. Evil Mom must have great power indeed to bring such light into the darkness.

And that was when the twins saw their escape route: Right next to the spot where the "boring stuff" box had been was a window. Quickly, the twins scrambled up the staircase of boxes. At the top box, Tou Bee got on all fours, and Tou Cher climbed from him to the top shelf. Then Tou Cher reached back down and pulled Tou Bee up until both brothers were next to the window. It was a small window, but they were thin. They turned the latch and opened it. Sunlight flooded the room.

"WHAT'S GOING ON IN HERE?" they heard Evil Mom roaring behind them right before both of them disappeared out the window.

• • •

[CHAPTER 6]

The Land
of the Frogs,
Halflings,
Wild Dogs,
and Basketball

[★]

They'd both done it! They'd outsmarted Evil Mom and solved a puzzle.

"But we still don't have our video game," complained Tou Cher.

"Maybe it wasn't even in the house," said Tou Bee. "Maybe Evil Mom ate it. *I* would eat it."

"Come on. A person can't swallow the disc. It would hurt. Duh."

That was true.

"But what if she's not really a person?" said Tou Bee.

Right now, they had to figure out what to do next.

In *The Awesome Adventures of Avery the Elf King*, whenever you were stuck, you could get advice from old people who were very wise.

"The Great Sage!" they blurted at the same time. That was the fun thing about being twins. You thought alike.

It was a long walk to the Great Sage's house, but if they wanted answers, they'd have to make the walk. The twins had never walked to the Great Sage's house by themselves before, but they had gone there many times with their mom—their *real* mom, not the evil one with fiery eyes who might have turned into a dragon.

But they remembered landmarks.

First, you had to pass the big green chair that only giants could sit on. Then you walked past a meadow. Beyond the meadow was a forest. Then, past the forest was the Great Sage's home.

"Why is this the land of frogs?" asked Tou Bee.

"Huh?"

"This place is called Frogtown," said Tou Bee pointing to the "Welcome to Frogtown" sign they were just passing. "But I've never seen any frogs around here."

"Maybe they're ghost frogs," said Tou Cher.

"No, I don't think so."

"How should I know why this is the land of frogs? Maybe there were swamps here."

But the whole time they lived in Frogtown, they had never seen swamps.

"There's the giant's chair," said Tou Cher as they passed an enormous green chair. The twins had seen the chair many times when crossing this area before. It looked like a wooden lawn chair, only super big. Once, their whole family—Mom, Dad, Noah, Payton, and the twins—even climbed onto the chair and sat on it, and still they had extra room. Real Mom often said that a giant sat there to watch over the city, but neither of the twins had seen the giant...yet.

"Let's hurry," said Tou Bee. "We've already seen too many scary things today. I don't want to meet a giant too."

The boys quickly ran past the chair.

They walked farther down the path, but there was still

no meadow.

"Are you sure we're going the right way?" asked Tou Bee.

"Yes," said Tou Cher. "Well, maybe. I don't know."

"Maybe we should go back. We can just search the house again."

"No," said Tou Cher. "We said we're going to see the Great Sage, and that's where we'll go. Just give me a minute to figure out where we are right now."

They paused in the middle of the path while Tou Cher closed his eyes and moved his head this way and that. He was using his big ears like an antenna to search for their path. Then...

"Did you hear that?" he whispered to Tou Bee.

"Hear what?"

"Close your eyes and listen."

Tou Bee closed his eyes. At first he didn't hear anything, but after a moment, he heard something faint.

Like a *bump-bump-bump*.

"Come on!" said Tou Cher.

"What if it's the giants?" asked Tou Bee, worried. But Tou Cher was already running toward the sound. The closer they got to the bump-bump-bump, the more clearly they could hear other sounds: people talking, laughing, and some high-pitched screeching.

"Look!" cried Tou Cher. "A sand dune."

A dune was like a beach. Tou Cher had learned that much from school.

"There are little halflings too," said Tou Cher.

"I think those are just little kids."

"I said they're halflings, so they're halflings," said Tou Cher. "Don't you remember when Avery met the halflings?"

Tou Bee did remember. Halflings were little people the size of children. Sometimes, they were from the fairy world.

The halflings were playing in the sand dunes.

"Let's ask them where the meadow is," said Tou Cher, and without waiting for an answer, he took off. Tou Bee followed as always.

"Hey," Tou Cher said to one halfling, "can you tell us where the meadow is? We need to find the Great Sage's house so we can get our video games back."

"Oy-oy-oy," said the halfling.

"I don't speak your language," said Tou Cher and turned to his brother. "Let's find another one. Maybe they'll speak English."

"Or maybe Hmong," said Tou Bee hopefully.

They spoke to another halfling, who answered them with "Buh-buh-buh." Another told them "Gah-gah-gah."

But they still had no idea where the meadow was.

"Hey, what are you doing?" came a voice.

Tou Bee and Tou Cher turned at the same time. It was a bigger creature—not quite as a big as a giant, but much bigger than them.

"That one must be one of the halfling's guardians," whispered Tou Bee. "Maybe we can ask—"

"Nah. That one looks angry," said Tou Cher. Taking his brother's hand, he turned away. They ran past the sand dunes and around a building. It was there they discovered what made the bump-bump-bump sounds.

"Those are creatures playing an ancient warrior's game," said Tou Cher.

"Those are kids just like us," said Tou Bee. "And they're playing basketball."

"They are *creatures*," insisted Tou Cher. "And look, we know one of them. In our world, that one goes by the name of 'Tommy.'"

Tou Bee rolled his eyes. They went to school with Tommy.

As they approached the creatures, Tou Bee called out, "Hey, Tommy!"

Tommy turned around. "Oh, hey, Tou Bee! Hey, Tou Cher! You guys wanna join us for a game?"

Tou Cher shrugged and Tou Bee looked unsure, but both of them joined the game with Tommy and his cousins.

They played two games, and even Tou Bee, who didn't like to be active, was having fun. Now he understood why people smiled and laughed when they played games outside. Who knew that basketball—or whatever ancient warrior game it was these creatures were playing—could be so fun when you played with more than one person?

While they rested before another game, Tommy asked, "So, whatcha been doing all summer?"

"Hello? Today's the first day of summer," said Tou Bee.

"And it's been boring so far," said Tou Cher. "We didn't do anything yet. What about you?"

"My cousins live around here, so we're gonna hang out at this park all summer and play games. Tomorrow, we're playing baseball out in the field."

"What field?" asked Tou Bee.

"Right over there," said Tommy.

Behind their benches was "over there," and "over there" was...

"The meadow!" cried the twins.

"Huh?" asked Tommy.

"We've been looking for the meadow," said Tou Bee.

"After the meadow is the forest," said Tou Cher, and sure enough, the boys could see a forest at the edge of the meadow.

"And after the forest is the Great Sage's house."

"Who?" asked Tommy.

"You don't play video games, do you?" asked the twins in unison.

"I got no time," said Tommy. "My family likes to play sports. My dad plays volleyball. My older brothers play flag football. And my cousins and I play...everything!"

"Well, this morning, an evil Mom took over our mom," said Tou Cher. "And she hid our video games. Now, we have to find them, but we don't know where they are."

"The Great Sage knows everything, and he'll tell us where the video games are," said Tou Bee.

"Are you gonna go looking for this...Great Sage, then?" asked Tommy.

"Nah. We can play with you guys for a while," said Tou Cher.

The three boys started walking toward the basketball court again when they heard screams. They looked around and saw one of the guardians gathering the halflings in his arms.

"Wild dog!" screamed the guardian.

And sure enough, a great big dog ran around the corner. The dog was large and gray. His mouth slobbered with saliva.

"Run!" screamed Tou Cher.

Tommy ran in the direction of his cousins. Tou Cher ran across the field toward the forest. It was only after he reached the forest that he realized he was alone. Where was Tou Bee?

• • •

[CHAPTER 7]

The Forest

[★]

Tou Cher hid in the shadows of the trees while he looked over the wide meadow. His eyes searched for his brother, but he couldn't find him anywhere. The meadow was big and wide like a green ocean. There was no place to hide. If Tou Bee had run toward the forest, Tou Cher would have seen him.

Though the basketball court was far away, he saw that it was empty now. Tommy and his cousins probably all went home. He couldn't see the sand dunes very well either, but the sand dunes were probably empty too. Tou Cher was bigger than the halflings, and still he was scared of the wild dog. The halflings were probably terrified.

That's what you get for running away first, said a voice in his head.

It was true. He was always running away first. He

always thought Tou Bee would follow his lead. It never occurred to him that Tou Bee might not follow him. Or maybe, this time, he *couldn't*.

Tou Cher closed his eyes and tilted his head so his ears could listen better. He moved his head this way and that, letting his ears search for any sounds of Tou Bee. There was nothing. Just the wind.

Maybe he should return home.

But no, he couldn't. The wild dog might still be out there waiting for him and the other kids. The only direction he could go was toward the Great Sage. Tou Bee would want that. Tou Bee would say, "We've already come this far. Let's keep going."

So, Tou Cher started walking. He would find his way to the Great Sage's house on his own. The Great Sage had many powers. Maybe he could even tell Tou Cher how to find his brother.

He walked and walked. There was no path in the

forest. He only walked where he thought he should. The forest was getting dark, and Tou Cher wondered if this was because there were just lots of trees or if nighttime was coming. In *The Awesome Adventures of Avery the Elf King*, the days were shorter than usual. You could play for one hour and suddenly it was nighttime, and different creatures came out at night. Like skeletons. Or bats. Or zombie animals.

Please don't let it be nighttime, he prayed. Nighttime meant the moon would come out. Mom always said, "Don't point at the moon or it will cut your ears."

Since he was often naughty, he would probably do something bad like point at it. He might not remember very many things about being Hmong, but he knew this story about the moon was something Hmong people believed "back in the day." One time, he even had a dream that the moon had visited him in the middle of the night ready to cut his ears—until Tou Bee told him what to do to protect himself.

Tou Bee told him, "You lick your fingers then wipe your spit on the back of your ears and say, 'Please, Moon, don't cut my ears.'"

Though it wasn't very dark yet, Tou Cher licked his index finger and began wiping it on the back of one ear.

That was when he felt a gentle *plop* on his face. He blinked his eyes and saw a bubble floating past him. And then another bubble, and another. Suddenly, there was a river of bubbles floating past him.

Tou Cher walked toward the bubbles. Who had created this river of bubbles? Was it a fairy queen?

If he found a fairy queen, he'd say, "Please bring back Tou Bee. If you bring back my brother, I'll promise to be good from now on. I'll listen in school and not get any more time-outs. I'll even let Tou Bee step on my back."

Soon, the river of bubbles disappeared and Tou Cher was afraid he wouldn't find the person who created them.

Then he heard a sound.

He was definitely not alone in the woods.

There was a *crunch-crunch-crunch* somewhere nearby. Softly, he walked toward the sound. It was a good thing it was summer right now. That meant there were no leaves crackling beneath his feet. As he walked, he hid himself behind trees.

Finally, he reached a small clearing in the forest and sucked in his breath.

There, sitting on the ground, was Tou Bee—eating potato chips, chomping on an apple, and sipping a juice box. At his feet was one of the bottles of bubbles he'd grabbed from the box of "fun stuff."

Immediately Tou Cher ran toward Tou Bee.

"Hey," he said.

"I was wondering where you went," said Tou Bee, still eating.

"Just walking," said Tou Cher, and he shrugged.

Sometimes, shrugging meant "I don't care," but it could also mean "I really missed you, but I don't want to look stupid so I'll just pretend like I don't care."

"Want some snacks?" asked Tou Bee.

Tou Cher joined him, grabbing a cookie and a juice box.

"Where did you go?" Tou Cher asked.

"When the wild dog came around the corner, Tommy ran back to his cousins. You ran toward the woods. I ran to our backpacks because I couldn't leave behind all our supplies."

"That was a dumb idea. A bag of chips isn't worth saving if you get bitten by a dog."

"But I didn't get bitten. One of the adults—I mean, one of the guardians of the halflings—grabbed the dog. He was a nice dog, just lost."

"How come I didn't see you run across the meadow?"

"I dunno. But I did. How come you're so serious all of

a sudden?" asked Tou Bee.

"I'm not," said Tou Cher. Before his brother could ask him more questions and make him admit he had been worried, he said, "Come on. Let's get out of these woods and find the Great Sage."

• • •

[CHAPTER 8]

The Bridge

[★]

As they walked farther through the forest, the trees got thinner and thinner and more sunlight came through.

"Look!" said Tou Cher. "We're almost out of the forest."

He could already see the paths beyond the trees.

"But, wait," said Tou Bee. "There's a roaring river ahead."

Tou Cher looked closer. "Oh, that's just a creek. We can probably just–"

"No, it's a roaring river," said Tou Bee matter-of-factly. "To get across, we'll need to build a bridge."

They looked around and found a long, heavy tree branch that had fallen to the ground. Tou Cher was about to drag it himself, but then he turned to Tou Bee and asked, "Can you help me?"

Together, they dragged the tree branch toward the

roaring river. With Tou Bee giving directions, they lifted the branch so one end stood tall, reaching toward the sky. Then, they pushed the branch to the other side of the river, where it landed with a *thump*. Though the branch was brown and some parts of it twisted like wrinkly arms, its body curved in an arc, like a rainbow.

"Yay! A bridge!" they both cheered.

Carefully, they walked across the tree-branch bridge. When they reached the other side, Tou Bee peered into the river.

"Whatcha looking at?" asked Tou Cher.

"Just wondering if there are crayfish in here like back in the day when Mom was a kid."

"*Are* there any crayfish?"

"Nah. But look, there are tadpoles," said Tou Bee.

"And frogs!" said Tou Cher.

Sure enough, there were frogs hopping around in the water and on the rocks.

"I knew there was a reason why this place was called Frogtown," said Tou Bee.

[CHAPTER 9]

The Great Sage

[★]

The Great Sage lived in a very plain brown house on a very plain street among very plain-looking people. He had once told the twins that this was all a disguise.

"When you are important," he said, "you need to hide out in the open."

The twins took this to mean you didn't hide at *all*.

When they knocked on the front door, an old woman opened the door.

"Is it just the two of you?" she asked, looking up and down the street. "Where's your mother?"

They couldn't very well tell her that an evil thing was pretending to be their mom, so Tou Cher said, "She just dropped us off for a bit."

"She'll be right back," added Tou Bee.

The old woman snorted.

Then Tou Bee said in Hmong, "Please, can we see Cousin

Meng?"

"He's upstairs," said the woman, letting them in. "Go tell him to wake up."

Once the boys were inside and alone, Tou Cher asked, "Why didn't you call him 'the Great Sage'?"

"Don't you remember? He told us to use code names. His code name is 'Cousin Meng.'"

"Oh," said Tou Cher.

They climbed up the stairs, then stopped in front of a door with a yellow poster on it that read "Go away."

Ignoring the poster, the brothers knocked on the door. After a few minutes, the Great Sage opened it. He was wearing his pajamas and holding a blue blanket around him.

The twins looked at him in awe. He was living every boy's dream: He got to wear his pajamas all day long. He woke up whenever he wanted. And he got to play video games all day, which was why he was the Great Sage. He had beaten nearly every video game the twins had heard of. He knew everything there was to know about life.

"Isn't it kinda early for you to be visiting?" asked the Great Sage.

"We have an emergency," said Tou Cher.

The Great Sage's voice became serious. "In that case, come inside."

The twins walked over piles of clothes and made their way to the Great Sage's bed, where they sat down. The Great Sage himself had a special throne right in front of his TV and three different video game systems. The twins couldn't wait for the day they could leave their clothes on the floor, not comb their hair, and get braces—just like the Great Sage.

"So what was such an emergency that you had to wake me up?" asked the Great Sage. Tou Bee saw that the clock on the wall read three o'clock, but he didn't say anything.

"Our mom took away our video games," said Tou Cher.

"Ah, man," groaned the Great Sage. "That was not cool."

"We've been looking for them everywhere, but we don't

know where they are," said Tou Bee.

"Parents just don't understand kids these days," said the Great Sage.

"But that's just the thing," said Tou Cher. "She's not our mom anymore. I'm sure she's turned into a creature or something."

"Our mom is nice," added Tou Bee. "She never takes away our games."

"And on the first day of summer vacation too," said the Great Sage, shaking his head in sympathy.

"We want to know what we should do," said Tou Cher. "You're old. You're almost fourteen. How do we find our video games?"

The Great Sage rubbed his chin and tilted his head like he was thinking. "Where have you looked?" he asked.

"In our living room, our kitchen, our dungeon—"

"Dude," interrupted the Great Sage. "You have a *dungeon*?"

"Some people call it a basement," explained Tou Bee.

"Oh."

"But they are not in any of those places."

"Have you looked in the most obvious place?" asked the Great Sage.

"What does 'obvious' mean?" Tou Cher whispered to Tou Bee.

But it was the Great Sage who answered. "It means the place that people don't look because they just think it won't be there, but it'll probably be there."

Noticing the twins' blank stares, the Great Sage said, "The dragon's lair."

"Ooohh."

"Don't you know by now? The first rule of video games is that you will always have to battle the dragon at the end. I'm willing to bet that whatever this..."

"We're calling her 'Evil Mom,'" said Tou Cher.

"I'm willing to bet that whatever this Evil Mom is, she's

probably turning into a dragon right now."

"That would explain the fiery eyes," Tou Bee said to Tou Cher.

"And the claw hands," said Tou Cher.

The Great Sage continued. "Now, dragons don't come to you. *You* go to *them*."

"But we're too little," said Tou Bee.

"If you're the chosen ones, you will beat them."

Tou Bee was afraid they weren't the chosen ones. They would probably just get eaten by the dragon. Or worse, they'd get in trouble when Mom became herself again.

"Here, I will give you two gifts as you continue your journey," said the Great Sage. "To you, Tou Bee, I give the gift of courage."

Tou Bee looked at the Great Sage's hands.

"But there's nothing there," he said.

"Courage is invisible," said the Great Sage. "You can't see it. You *feel* it."

Tou Bee didn't feel anything but weird.

"Look, do you want courage or not?"

Tou Bee was silent because that was more polite than saying "no."

"Fine, fine, fine," said the Great Sage. "How about this instead?"

The Great Sage rose from his throne and removed his blue blanket. He held the blanket out to Tou Bee.

"To you, Tou Bee, I give my blanket of invisibility."

"What does it do?" asked Tou Bee.

"Duh. It makes you *invisible*."

"Then how come we can see you?" asked Tou Cher.

"Because it only works if you cover it over your whole body. How do you think I've played video games all these years? I hide underneath my invisibility blanket every time my mom knocks on my door."

The twins nodded in understanding and awe. There was always so much you could learn from the Great Sage. Tou

Bee happily took the blanket of invisibility.

"What about me?" asked Tou Cher. "What do I get?"

The Great Sage turned to Tou Cher and said, "To you, Tou Cher, I give the gift of strength."

"Cool. So then I can lift heavy stuff now?"

"Uh...it can also mean that you are stronger as a person."

"So then I *still* can't lift heavy stuff?"

"Fine, fine, fine," said the Great Sage. "To you, I give the gift of this...wooden spoon."

From behind him, the Great Sage pulled out a wooden spoon and slapped it in Tou Cher's hand.

"What can it do?" asked Tou Cher.

"If you ever get stuck, spin this spoon around your head three times, and it will cook up an idea for you."

Tou Cher stared at the spoon in confusion. "But can I hit the dragon with it?"

"You cannot beat the dragon with strength alone. You need this," said the Great Sage, tapping his head.

"A big head? Tou Bee has a big head," said Tou Cher.

"Brains. You need *brains*," said the Great Sage. "You need to be smart and sneaky."

At that, the twins looked at each other and smiled brightly. They both knew Tou Bee was smart and Tou Cher was sneaky. They should be all right then, shouldn't they?

"Now, if that is all..." The Great Sage turned away toward his video games.

"Before we leave, we need to give you a thank-you gift we brought," said Tou Bee. He opened his backpack and pulled out the chicken wings he'd dumped in there earlier.

"Wow! Great gift!" exclaimed the Great Sage. "I haven't eaten anything at all today."

The twins smiled proudly because they had brought the right gift for the Great Sage. Then they made their way back home. They had some video games to find and a dragon to fight.

• • •

[CHAPTER 10]

The Dragon's Lair

[★]

The house was suspiciously quiet when the twins returned. The kitchen had been cleaned up from that morning. They tiptoed into the living room. The ninja was sleeping on the couch, his belly moving up and down. With his mask off and his chubby cheeks showing, he didn't look so scary.

Tou Cher motioned for Tou Bee to be quiet, and Tou Bee nodded back.

They made their way up the stairs, careful to avoid the one stair that creaked. They looked down the hallway. No one. They passed by their bedroom and saw that it was empty. They passed the bathroom. Empty. They were walking past their sister Payton's room when the door opened. Payton stood in the doorway, still wearing her princess dress from the morning. Luckily, her feet were bare. Maybe the dragon had taken away her plastic

Princess shoes. Thank goodness. They didn't need any sounds alerting the dragon.

"You two are in *big* trouble," said Payton.

"Quiet down," whispered Tou Cher.

"Where is everyone?" asked Tou Bee.

"It's nap time," said Payton. "But I can't sleep. I want my iPod."

"We might be able to get it back," said Tou Bee. "But we'll need your help."

After he told Payton to go back to her room, he and Tou Cher crept to the last room down the hall. The door was ajar, and as they pushed it they were glad when it opened without a creak.

On the huge bed in the middle of the room, they saw that Evil Mom had indeed turned into a dragon since the last time they saw her. The dragon was in a deep sleep. Instead of Mom's bare feet, the dragon's curled talons dangled over the side of the bed. Her dark hair went everywhere, and she snored loudly. Every time the dragon snored, it felt like the room took one big breath in and one big breath out.

Silently, the twins circled the room. The dragon's bed was so high it reached their necks, but they knew there was one step on the side of the bed that helped you get up and down. As they came around to the other side of the bed, they got a better view of the dragon's face. But more importantly, they saw its claws curled underneath something beneath the pillows.

"Look!" whispered Tou Cher. "Our video games are right there next to the dragon."

They hadn't expected that. They were hoping the games would be somewhere in the dragon's lair, not actually underneath the dragon's head.

The brothers retreated from the dragon's lair and spoke farther down the hallway.

"We'll never get the games," whispered Tou Bee.

"But we gotta try," said Tou Cher. "Use your head."

So, Tou Bee *thought* and *thought* and *thought* about it. Finally, he said, "Use your spoon!"

"Huh?" asked Tou Cher.

"The Great Sage said if you're ever stuck, spin the spoon around your head three times and an idea will come to you."

"He did?" asked Tou Cher.

"Don't you ever listen?" Tou Bee sighed.

"No. Why do you think I always get time-outs in school?"

Still, Tou Cher took out the wooden spoon and spun it around his head one time. He felt nothing. He spun it around a second time. Still nothing. Then he spun it around a third time and—

"I've got an idea!" Tou Bee said in excitement.

Tou Cher was relieved, because he still didn't have any ideas.

Tou Bee led Tou Cher into Payton's room, where he told both of them his plans. Then the boys headed toward the dragon's lair. They sprinkled the last of their potato chips up and down the hallway. Inside the lair, they quietly took the yarn they had found earlier and wound it in and out and around the lair. The room was semi-dark, with all the windows partly covered. They hoped this meant the dragon would not see the little web they created. Then Tou Cher used his strength to push the bed stool a few feet down from where it usually was.

Ready to put their plan into action, Tou Cher signaled Payton down the hallway, then returned to a small corner in the room where Tou Bee was waiting with the Great Sage's invisibility blanket. They gave each other one last look, then pulled the blanket over their heads. Now invisible, they waited for the dragon to wake up.

• • •

[CHAPTER 11]

Smart and Sneaky

[★]

It began with screaming, lots of screaming. Payton was definitely bratty sometimes, and she sure could scream. From down the hallway her screams echoed throughout the house, awakening the dragon, who rose from her slumber and roared.

The dragon was fearsome with orange and hot-pink scales, and dark hair mussed everywhere. The dragon got off her perch and…fell onto the floor in a loud *thunk*. She roared some more, and Tou Bee and Tou Cher were glad they were hidden safely away behind an invisibility blanket. They did not want to confront her in her wrath.

The dragon rose from the ground and charged toward the door, but she got caught up in the web of yarn.

"What the heck—" and again the dragon fell down

trying to stand up.

Tou Cher was tempted to say "Yes!" out loud, but he held his excitement in check.

Down the hallway, Payton continued to scream.

The dragon finally stumbled out of the room. As she lumbered out the hall, the twins heard the dragon's growl. She must be stepping on the potato chips just now. That would hurt with no shoes on.

Quickly, Tou Bee and Tou Cher shed the invisibility blanket and ran toward the bed. Tou Cher climbed the bed step and felt underneath the pillows. There, hidden not-so-very well, was *The Awesome Adventures of Avery the Elf King* along with other video games and Payton's iPod. Tou Cher grabbed the games and threw them down to Tou Bee. Then he grabbed the iPod and slid off the bed.

"We did it! We did it!" he chanted.

Tou Bee started to smile and celebrate, but his face

fell suddenly as the dragon stood in the doorway, nostrils flaring, hair askew, and mouth huffing and puffing.

"So, you've returned!" she roared right before she slammed the door shut behind her.

"Quick!" Tou Cher yelled. "The invisibility blanket!"

He and Tou Bee threw the invisibility blanket over their heads. From beneath the blanket, they saw the dragon walking around the room pulling up all the window blinds. They remembered a stage from *The Awesome Adventures of Avery the Elf King* where the bad guy cornered Avery and he had to fight back. This must be like that scene.

Light flooded the room. Once the room was fully lit, the dragon stomped toward them. Suddenly she stopped to pull a piece of potato chip off the bottom of her foot. Then she began tearing away the yarn.

Tou Bee shivered.

"You have the power of courage now," Tou Cher whispered beside him. "Don't be afraid."

"But I didn't take the courage when the Great Sage gave it to me," worried Tou Bee.

"Well, that doesn't matter because she can't see us anyway," said Tou Cher.

Right then and there, the blanket was plucked from their heads and the dragon stared down at both of them.

"But I thought this was an invisibility blanket," said Tou Cher while Tou Bee muttered under his breath, "Oh, Cousin Meng..."

"I'm much stronger and much smarter than you think! I can see through your little games!" roared the dragon.

"You have the power of strength now," Tou Bee said to Tou Cher. "Don't be afraid. You can fight for us."

"Uh...I didn't accept that from the Great Sage either,"

said Tou Cher.

Tou Cher had heard of people shaking in their boots, but he didn't know what that meant until now. He didn't think he could fight a dragon.

"So, you found your precious video games, did you?" asked the dragon in a quiet, creepy voice.

The twins swallowed and held their video games closer to their hearts, even though right now they both just wished they could run away.

"You think you can just walk away and nothing will happen?" asked the dragon, her voice rising.

"Well, we didn't know what we would do once we got our video games back," said Tou Bee.

"We were hoping we could just play them," said Tou Cher.

"Today, you two created a huge mess in the kitchen. You created an even larger mess in the basement. Then you ran off to who-knows-where. And just now you made me think your sister was in trouble. You made me fall off the bed and hurt myself. You did all this just for the precious video games, and you think I will just say 'yes'?"

There was a pause as the twins thought about it. Then Tou Cher said, "Well, you're not really our mom. You're a dragon, aren't you?"

"Excuse me?" roared the dragon.

"Our mom would never yell at us or take away our games," said Tou Bee.

"And, besides," Tou Cher continued, "if you were really our mom, you wouldn't want us to tell Dad later that you lost us for a few hours, would you?"

The dragon narrowed her eyes.

"You're a sneaky one, aren't you?" she said to Tou Cher.

"Maybe we could make a deal," said Tou Bee. "What if we helped you clean up our mess and we promised to be good? Would you let us play our video games tomorrow?"

Tou Bee hoped that was a smart thing to say.

The dragon kneeled down so she could see them at eye level. She thought about their words for a moment. She looked like she wanted to huff and puff.

Instead, right before their eyes, the dragon's claws turned into hands, her talons into feet, her hot pink and orange scales into a sweat suit, and her fiery eyes became a soft brown again.

In the end, it was Mom, not the dragon or Evil Mom, who said, "Deal."

• • •

[CHAPTER 12]

The End
of the First Day of
Summer Vacation

[★]

That evening, the whole family sat down to a dinner of pancakes, noodles, Hmong sausages, rice, and pepper. Dad looked at everything suspiciously, but he said nothing as he ate his dinner.

After a while, he asked, "So, how was the first day of summer vacation?"

"Mom told us we could only play with our imaginations today," said Payton, eating a big bite of pancake and syrup.

"Really?" said Dad. "And what did you do?"

"I was a princess, but I wasn't pretending."

"A princess? Well, that's a surprise," he chuckled.

"I was a ninja," said Noah. "And then I slept all afternoon."

"And what about you boys?" Dad asked, turning to Tou Bee and Tou Cher. Maybe it was *his* imagination, but he thought he saw Mom suck in her breath.

"We had the best day ever," said Tou Bee.

"Mom turned into a dragon," said Tou Cher.

"She did?" Here, Dad turned to Mom and gave her a wink. Mom just gave him one of her fake smiles.

"And we had to save her," said Tou Bee.

"And get back our video games," said Tou Cher.

"So we packed supplies—"

"Searched the dungeon—"

"Went through the Land of the Frogs—"

"Spoke with some halflings—"

"Played basketball—"

"You mean, a warrior game—"

"Saw a wild dog—"

"Got lost in the forest—"

"Talked to the Great Sage—"

"Then we came home and defeated the dragon—"

"And brought Mom back home."

"Wow, you had a quite an adventure," said Dad. "And you did all this in one day?"

The twins nodded.

"You two sure have a great imagination!"

"But it *wasn't* our imagination," said Tou Cher. "It was *real*."

Dad just smiled. Then he turned to Mom and asked, "So, what are your plans for tomorrow?"

Mom just gave Dad an I'm-not-going-to-tell-you-what-I'm-thinking smile and ate her pepper.

• • •

About the Author

 May Lee-Yang is a Hmong American playwright, poet, prose writer, and performance artist. She was born in Ban Vinai, a refugee camp in Thailand, following the Secret War in Laos. Nine months after her birth, her family resettled in St. Paul, Minnesota, where she lives to this day.

She has been hailed by *Twin Cities Metro Magazine* as "on the way to becoming one of the most powerful and colorful voices in local theater." Her writing has been published in *Asian American Plays for a New Generation* (Temple University Press), *How Do I Begin? A Hmong American Literary Anthology* (Heyday Press), *Bamboo Among the Oaks: Contemporary Writing by Hmong Americans* (Minnesota Historical Society Press), *Water~Stone Literary Review, The Saint Paul Almanac*, and others.

Her theater-based works have been presented at Mu Performing Arts, the Center for Hmong Arts and Talent (CHAT), Out North Theater, the 2011 National Asian American Theater Festival, the Minnesota Fringe Festival, and others. Her show *Confessions of a Lazy Hmong Woman* has been toured nationally and was remixed in the Hmong language.

She has received grants and awards from the Bush Foundation, the Minnesota State Arts Board, the National Performance Network, Midwestern Voices and Visions, the Playwright Center, and the Loft Literary Center. She received her B.A. in English from the University of Minnesota–Twin Cities.

Some fun facts about May are that she loves chocolate cake, chubby kids, and karaoke. She also currently has at least thirty-nine nieces and nephews (with more on the way).

For more info about her work, go to www.lazyhmongwoman.com.

About the Illustrator

Anne Sawyer-Aitch (pronounced like the letter "H") is a puppeteer and stilt-walker. She has worked with companies such as Heart of the Beast, Open Eye Figure Theatre, Chicks on Sticks, Artstart, and her own company, Magic Lantern Puppet Theatre. She is a recipient of awards from the Jim Henson Foundation, the Puppeteers of America, and the Metropolitan Regional Arts Council. She is the author/illustrator of the children's book *Nalah and the Pink Tiger*, which is based on her little niece. Anne creates puppet pieces of all kinds: parade floats, giant stilt puppets, and intricate color shadow shows. She is a Minnesota State Arts Board Roster Artist, teaching puppetry arts all over the state. She lives in Minneapolis with her computer genius husband and a pack of imaginary dogs.

[PHOTO BY KAREN HASELMANN]

COUNCIL ON
ASIAN PACIFIC
MINNESOTANS
A STATE AGENCY SINCE 1985

MINNESOTA
Humanities Center

CLEAN
WATER
LAND &
LEGACY
AMENDMENT

This work is funded with money from the Arts and Cultural Heritage Fund that was created with the vote of the people of Minnesota on November 4, 2008.